LITTLE STONE BUDDHA

Little Stone Buddha

BY K. T. HAO

ILLUSTRATED BY
GIULIANO FERRI

Translated by Annie Kung

PURPLE BEAR BOOKS
NEW YORK

High above the Nine Tall Mountains a thunderbolt flashed across the sky. It struck a rocky cliff and sent a large stone tumbling down the mountain.

The stone rolled and rolled and finally came to a stop beside a mountain path.

For many years afterward, people would stop to rest on the stone. It seemed to hold a mysterious power that energized even the weariest traveler in just a few moments. As time went by it took on a curious shape.

One day a stonemason passed by. As he studied the stone, he had a brilliant idea. Inspired, he set to work with his chisel and hammer and transformed the stone into a statue of a little Buddha.

That night, beneath the glow of the full moon, the little
Buddha basked in silvery light. And just at dawn, as the first
ray of sunlight shone on his face, he moved! He yawned
deeply, stretched wide, and chanted a long oooommmm,
as though wakening from a thousand-year sleep.

Curious, Little Stone Buddha explored
the mountainside. He watched butterflies
flittering in the warm breeze, fish swimming
past in the stream. He listened to the roar
of the waterfall, and smiled happily at
how beautiful the world was.

From then on, Little Stone Buddha wandered the mountain paths, always looking for someone who needed his help. When travelers, hot and tired from their journeys, stopped to rest, he would restore them with a cool breeze. When they tripped, Little Stone Buddha would catch them before they fell.

Even though Little Stone Buddha was invisible when he was moving around, people sensed his presence and his blessings. In gratitude, they would leave simple offerings of food and drink in front of the statue.

One afternoon, Little Stone Buddha lay beneath a tree, enjoying the birds singing above him. Suddenly, their song turned to shrill warning calls. Three hunters appeared over the hill, chasing after a little fox.

One hunter took aim and shot an arrow right at the fox.
But the arrow stopped, frozen in mid-flight. Little Stone
Buddha had caught it just in time!

With a wave of his hand, Little Stone Buddha sent the three hunters tumbling into a heap. Before they could stand and take aim again, the fox raced off to the woods, scampering to safety through the fallen leaves.

Winter came and snow covered the mountainside.
Little Stone Buddha sat quietly, appreciating how the
bright red sho-tao offering stood out against the
white snow. It was almost too pretty to eat.

A little fox ran up to Little Stone Buddha—the same little fox he had rescued from the hunters. The fox had been out looking for food and hungrily eyed the sho-tao.

Just then, another little fox appeared, and soon the two were quarreling over the sho-tao.

Little Stone Buddha stood up. "Do not quarrel," he said. "You may each have half of my sho-tao and then let's play together."

What better game on a snowy day than a snowball fight!
A snowball to the left and one to the right. Little Stone
Buddha and the foxes had a wonderful time.

Suddenly they heard someone coming. Little Stone Buddha quickly sat down, as still and frozen as a statue. The two foxes stood on either side of him, not moving a muscle so that they, too, looked like statues.

The traveler who had come to worship Little Stone Buddha offered him a sho-tao and left two more—one for each of the little foxes.

From that day on, throughout the Nine Tall Mountains, foxes were honored as Little Stone Buddha's followers. They were so revered that no one ever hunted foxes again.

Buddhism began in India in the 5th century BC.
It spread across Asia and is now considered to be the oldest and
most widespread of all world religions. The man who was to become
the Buddha was born a prince named Siddhartha Gautama in what
is now part of Nepal. He abandoned his privileged background
to seek enlightenment and devoted the rest of his life
to self-sacrifice and good deeds.

One of the offerings made to the Little Stone Buddha
in this story is sho-tao, which literally translates into "long-life peach."
It is a bunlike dessert generally served at birthday or other banquets
in China. It is made of flour dough, shaped into a peach,
tinted with red food coloring, filled with sweet
red bean paste, and then steamed.

Text copyright © 2003 by K. T. Hao
Illustrations copyright © 2003 by Giuliano Ferri
English translation copyright © 2005 by Purple Bear Books Inc.

First published in Taiwan in 2003 by Grimm Press
First English-language edition published in 2005 by Purple Bear Books Inc., New York
For more information about our books visit our website, purplebearbooks.com

Library of Congress Cataloging-in-Publication Data is available.
This edition prepared by Cheshire Studio.

ISBN 1-933327-01-4 (trade edition)
1 3 5 7 9 TE 10 8 6 4 2
ISBN 1-933327-05-7 (library edition)
1 3 5 7 9 LE 10 8 6 4 2
Printed in Taiwan